The Monster Under Your Bed is Just a Story in Your Head

Printed in the United States of America

First Printing, 2017

ISBN 978-0-692-80006-5

Neurosculpting® Institute Publishing
An imprint of Ripple Effect LLC
1245 E. Colfax Ave, Suite 207
Denver, CO 80205

www.NeurosculptingInstitute.com

The Monster Under Your Bed is Just a Story in Your Head

By: Lisa Wimberger
Illustrated by: Zoe Jay

Neurosculpting® Institute Publishing
Denver, Colorado

For my daughter, Havana. May you always remember the power of choice.

Peanut gets ready for bed.

She brushes her teeth, gets into her snuggly pajamas and climbs into her warm bed.

All is well.

But then Peanut does something she seems to do a lot lately. She makes a little visit to the library in her mind. She goes here often to look through memories and stories that live there. She likes to look for the perfect bedtime story to tell herself.

Strangely, the library is a very big place inside her child-sized head. It's amazing how so many memories and stories can fit inside. She's greeted by the librarian Mr. Hippocampus, who is always there to help her retrieve her bedtime story. Peanut calls him Mr. Hippo, which sounds like it's short for hippopotamus. But what's really strange is that he doesn't look like a hippopotamus at all, rather he looks like a Sea Horse!

Mr. Hippo greets Peanut in the usual way, with a big warm smile and a hearty, "Welcome to the library of your stories! Which story would you like to read today?"

Mr. Hippo is so helpful anytime Peanut wanted to remember something he's always there helping.

"Would you like the story of the time you got a big hug from your mother? Or would you prefer the story of the time when you ate so much yummy food your belly made you happy?" asks Mr. Hippo.

Even though Peanut really loves the stories that make her feel warm and fuzzy, it seems that before she knows it she asks for a very different sort of story: the one about the big scary monster that lives under her bed.

Now Peanut **knows** that a big monster could never fit under her bed, and even though her parents tell her many times that it isn't real, she spends a lot of time feeling scared of this story anyway. The more she feels scared of it and thinks about it, the more important Mr. Hippo thinks it is. Wanting to be a helpful librarian, Mr. Hippo keeps this important story handy and waiting for Peanut any time she visits the library.

Mr. Hippo simply wants to do a good job, giving Peanut the stories she asks for most.

With the familiar but made-up monster story in hand, Peanut heads for the door where she encounters her old friend Miss Amy, short for Miss Amygdala, which Peanut could never pronounce correctly.

Miss Amy looks strangely like a plump almond. These library folks sure look peculiar. Miss Amy opens the door for her and asks, "Which story did you get today, Peanut?"

Peanut holds up the Monster Under the Bed story.

"Oh, that one comes with all sorts of things to make it more interesting. Wait here and I'll get them for you."

Miss Amy dashes away and quickly returns with a bag of things. She pulls out a coat that looks way too small, but she stuffs Peanut into it anyway. When she buttons it too tightly Peanut can't breathe so well.

Her arms feel tense and frozen in the very snug sleeves. This doesn't feel good. And then Miss Amy takes out a too-small hat and jams Peanut's head into it. It feels too tight and gives her a headache. Yuck, this doesn't feel good AT ALL. But just when she thinks she can leave to read her story Miss Amy takes out one more item. A necklace! She places it on Peanut's neck but it, too, is very small and pinches a bit so that Peanut can't swallow well.

Miss Amy says, "Now you are ready to read the story and feel all of the feelings that make this monster story seem real."

Peanut feels tight, stuck, unable to breathe easily or swallow, with a terrible headache. Yes, Peanut feels stress and FEAR, and this seems very familiar when she thinks about each time she reads this very same story. Even though Miss Amy helps her feel this way, she is not a mean person. She is just doing her job to make the story more real. But she gives Peanut some great advice before she leaves.

"Peanut, remember that once you stop reading this story I'll take back all of the items and you can go back to feeling calm, breathing deeply, and thinking clearly…like the way you feel when you aren't feeling FEAR."

Peanut asks, "When will that be?"

"Whenever you are ready to read a different story!" answered Miss Amy.

Peanut wonders why she keeps reading the scary story instead of some of the ones that make her feel good. And precisely when she thinks this Miss Amy adds, "Sometimes the scary stories are easier to retrieve because they come with strong feelings and strong feeling stories are filed up front in the library so Mr. Hippo doesn't have to go too far to get them for you."

Peanut stops for a moment and asks, "What if I don't want to read this story anymore but it's up front? How do I get a different story to be filed up front so Mr. Hippo gets that one easily?"

Miss Amy smiles her biggest, warmest smile.

"That's a GREAT question and one of life's most precious secrets. Do you think you are ready to learn such a precious secret?"

With all her heart Peanut nods yes.

Miss Amy steps in closer, kneels down, and takes Peanut's hands.

"Listen carefully," she says. "You have read this particular story many times. The more you do anything the easier it is to do that thing. So getting this story and feeling scared is now easy for you. That's exactly what happens when you practice being scared. So now you have to *practice* feeling safe, warm and cozy. You have to choose a different story and tell it to yourself many times for it to be practiced enough to be easy. You have to stop all throughout the warm story and ask what types of things can your body feel during this story. Let's try that together."

"When you think of the story of when you got your biggest hug what did your belly feel like?"

Peanut takes a moment and answers, "Warm, calm, and full."

"Great," says Miss Amy. "Now let's spend a few moments with our eyes closed practicing feeling warm, calm and full in the belly."

After a few moments of imagining this, Peanut begins to feel it!

"What else might you feel when getting your biggest hug?"

Peanut answers, "Protected and safe and soft in my chest."

And then Miss Amy asks Peanut to close her eyes and practice that.

After a few more minutes Peanut is breathing deeply and feeling safe.

Suddenly she realizes she is no longer holding the Monster story. The too-small coat is gone, her necklace and hat disappear.

Confused, she asks what happened.

Miss Amy answers, "You wrote a new story and practiced it. You were so busy doing that you couldn't hold on to the scary story so Mr. Hippo came and filed it on a back shelf. How do you feel now?"

Peanut answers, "I feel good. I'm not scared."

Miss Amy gives her a big hug and says, "Will you come back tomorrow before bed and retrieve this new story we wrote together today?"

"Yes, I will!" replies Peanut. "But how should I ask for it?"

"Let's give it a name or a favorite color so that when you come back you can tell Mr. Hippo how to find it for you."

"Ok, I'll call it Purple Yummy!" she answers.

Miss Amy speaks softly and says, "Wonderful, I'll look forward to making your goodie bag for Purple Yummy then!"

She leans in to give Peanut a kiss on the top of her head and before you know it Peanut is fast asleep.

The End

Parent Guide and Practices

Sometimes helping our children deal with complex emotions can be confusing and difficult. This story is full of embedded Neurosculpting® practices designed to help your child envision and create their stories differently in a self-directed manner. The next time you read this to your child, try pausing where Peanut describes what she feels and ask your child to describe how he or she feels during those types of thoughts. This interactive dialogue helps bring awareness to the emotional process.

Here is a list of easy practices you can do to help your child navigate the contracting effects of complex emotions.

1. Shake your bodies together (shake it off!)
   Shaking vigorously even for a few short minutes helps release contraction in the muscles, some of which can hold emotions and the physical patterns of fear and defense.
2. Practice deep breathing
   Long breaths in and out help signal the nervous system to being relaxing. An even longer exhale can help relax us even faster. You can help your child by having them imagine they are blowing out many candles on a cake. A few minutes of this encourages a rest-and-digest state for the nervous system.
3. Entrain to the positive
   Help your child make a list of the things they notice in their surroundings that make them feel safe, supported, or nurtured. This can help the brain down-regulate a hyper-vigilant stress and survival response.
4. Cultivate gratitude
   Help your child identify one or two things they are grateful for. Encourage them to tell you why they are grateful. Gratitude has a measurable correlation to activity in the front of the brain which is an asset in emotional regulation. Since the front of the brain is not yet matured in children, this sort of gentle exercise helps strengthen it.
5. Role model

Practice these same exercises with your child so you can role model a set of tools for dealing simply with complex stress states. You just might find some relief as well!

Nutrition for Stress Regulation

What we eat, or don't eat, primes our relationship to emotional regulation. Our brains need three things to function properly and help us navigate the world gracefully. When any one of these is missing from our main diet we will have a deficiency in vital brain resources. When these are present in our children's diets in a balanced way, emotional regulation becomes easier.

1. Healthy carbohydrates
   Vegetables and fruits are prime choices.
2. Healthy fats
   Fish and oils and omegas from coconut, olives, nuts, seeds, and avocados are prime choices.
3. Healthy proteins
   Free range grass-fed animal products and/or vegetarian sources like beans and nuts are prime choices.

Want to learn more about how to regulate stress and emotions in the body and mind with the trademarked Neurosculpting® process? Visit us for in person, online, or download classes at the Neurosculpting® Institute. www.neurosculptinginstitute.com

About the author:

Lisa Wimberger is a mom, wife, musician, dancer and founder of the Neurosculpting® Institute in Denver. She has devoted her life to teaching and empowering people to navigate stress and trauma with grace and hope. To contact Lisa email her at Lisa@neurosculptinginstitute.com

Made in the USA
San Bernardino, CA
09 May 2017